photo is of a statue of Judah Loew of Prague, the legendary creator of the Golem. This monument to Loew by Ladislaus Saloun stands today in Prague near the Town Hall. Photo by Lois Badgero.

THE GOLEM LEGEND

ORIGINS AND IMPLICATIONS

BYRON L. SHERWIN

UNIVERSITY
PRESS OF
AMERICA

LANHAM • NEW YORK • LONDON

University Press of America,™ Inc.

4720 Boston Way
Lanham, MD 20706

3 Henrietta Street
London WC2E 8LU England

Library of Congress Cataloging in Publication Data

Sherwin, Byron L.
  The Golem legend.

  Bibliography: p.
  1. Golem. I. Title.
BM531.S54   1984   398'.45'089924   84-21948
ISBN 0-8191-4402-9 (alk. paper)
ISBN 0-8191-4403-7 (pbk. : alk. paper)

For my mother
  who gave me life
    and
For my son
  who gives me hope

The publication of this work was made possible by grants from the Anshe Emet Synagogue Publication Fund, The Idea Exchange, and the Cohn Scholars Fund. The author is grateful for their support of his endeavors.

Also by Byron L. Sherwin:

Judaism: The Way of Sanctification
Encountering the Holocaust
Abraham Joshua Heschel
Garden of the Generations
Mystical Theology and Social Dissent:
    The Life and Works of Judah Loew of Prague
Jerzy Kosinski: Literary Alarmclock

"The Golem? I've heard talk of it a lot. What do you know about the Golem . . .?

"Who can say he knows anything about the Golem? . . .

"Always they treat it as a legend, till something happens and it turns into actuality once more . . . ."

From
The Golem
by
Gustav Meyrink

Few post-biblical Jewish legends – if any – have evoked the interest or have provoked the imagination of Jews and of non-Jews as has the legend of the Golem. In his retelling of the Golem legend, novelist Elie Wiesel characterizes the Golem as "the most fascinating creature in Jewish lore and fantasy." No other Jewish legend has been as influential in inspiring literary works, artistic expression and scientific speculation as has the Golem legend.

The legend of the Golem has evoked novels by Gustav Meyrink, Max Brod and Abraham Rothberg as well as poetry by Hugo Salus and Jorge Luis Borges. It has stimulated drama by Rudolph Lothar and H. Leivick. Eugene d'Albert composed an opera based upon the Golem legend, and Joseph Achron's *Golem Suite* reflects the legend in music and dance. Short story writers such as David Frischmann, I. L. Peretz, I. B. Singer and Cynthia Ozick have retold the story of the Golem. Science fiction writers as Avram Davidson have been intrigued with the Golem. Early film makers made movies about the Golem. Even comic books introduced characters such as the "Galactic Golem." Children's games such as "Dungeons and Dragons" include a Golem.

There is some evidence that Goethe's ballad "The Sorcerer's Apprentice," and Mary Shelley's *Frankenstein* were influenced by the Golem legend. Norbert Wiener, the "father of cybernetics," explores the relationship between humans and machines in a work entitled, *God and Golem, Inc.* Norbert Wiener identifies the relationship between people and machines as being one of the central problems presently facing us. Wiener describes the machine as "the modern counterpart of the Golem." *Time* magazine compared the first "test-tube baby" to the creation of the Golem.

In dedicating a computer at the Weizmann Institute in Israel, Gershom Scholem named the computer "Golem No. One," observing that the computer is a modern form of the Golem. Jay Gonen, in his *Psychohistory of Zionism*, describes Zionism and the State of Israel as political permutations of the Golem legend. Like the Golem, Gonen observes, Israel was created as a means of protecting the physical safety of Jews through the use of physical power.

It is almost as if the Golem does not wish to rest eternally in the attic of the synagogue in Prague where legend places its final repose. The Golem returns in a variety of forms to confront us. Many of the moral, psychological and spiritual problems that we wrestle with today seem to have been anticipated by the Golem legend. Daily newspapers and weekly magazines carry stories of modern Golems — the benefits they offer, and the risks they represent. As the motifs found in early legend and recent science fiction increasingly become historical fact and daily experience, the insights and implications of the Golem legend become increasingly pertinent.

This study will focus on two questions:

What is the legend of the Golem?

What are the contemporary implications of the Golem legend?

To answer the first question one must review the development of the Golem legend in classical Jewish literature. The place to begin is a text found in the Talmud:

Raba said: If the righteous desired it, they could create worlds, for it is written: "But your iniquities have distinguished between you and your God" (Isaiah 59:2).

Rabbah created a man and sent him to Rabbi Zera. Rabbi Zera spoke to him (i.e., to the artificially created man), but received no answer. Thereupon, he (i.e., Rabbi Zera) said to him (i.e., to the artificially created man): You are from the companions. Return to your dust.

Rabbi Hanina and Rabbi Oshaia spent every Sabbath eve studying the *Sefer Yetzirah (The Book of Creation)*, by means of which they created a third-grown calf which they ate (*Sanhedrin* 65b).

Raba's statement introduces two crucial notions. First, that human beings have the potentiality to create worlds. (Contrast, however, the rabbinic text that states: If all the creatures in the world gathered together to make a single gnat and *put a soul into it,* they would not succeed. *Sifre Deuteronomy* #32 to Deuteronomy 6:5, and, compare *Genesis Rabbah* 39:14). Second, that sin prevents humans from fully manifesting the creative abilities that they potentially share with God. Raba seems to be saying that the feature that we share with God is our creative ability. God is a creator. We are created in the divine image. We strive for *imitatio dei.* Therefore, when we are creators, we are most like God; we are most clearly in His image. Sin makes us un-Godlike. Sin separates us from that image. Sin stifles our potentiality to be creative.

It is noteworthy that Raba never questions the propriety of human beings striving to be Godlike, to be creators. Raba does not question the propriety of creating worlds or of creating artificial life. For Raba, and apparently for Rabbah, the creation of worlds and the creation of artificial life is not a usurpation of God's role of creator, but is rather a fulfillment of the human potential to become a creator. While other traditions and other religions considered the creation of artificial beings to be demonic (see e.g. Faust), Jewish tradition embraced, and even encouraged, such creative activity.

The term "Golem" is not found in our text; nevertheless, the text represents the first record of a creation of a Golem by a human being, and it was so understood by future commentaries. In fact, in many versions of the Golem legend the term "Golem" is not used. In a number of post-talmudic texts, the Golem is referred to as "a man created by means of the *Sefer Yetzirah*." This description of the Golem, as we shall see, is rooted in the commentaries to the text under examination.

Perhaps because the text speaks of Rabbi Hanina's and Rabbi Oshaia's ability to create a calf by means of the *Sefer Yetzirah*, or, perhaps because he was in possession of early traditions regarding the creation of an artificial person, Rashi interprets "Rabbah created a man" to mean "Rabbah created a man by means of the *Sefer Yetzirah* in which he learned the letter-combinations of the Name" (also see Rashi to *Sanhedrin* 67b). Whether the *Sefer Yetzirah* that Rashi refers to is identical to the *Sefer Yetzirah* mentioned in the talmudic text is open to some doubt. Nevertheless, Rashi and the later commentaries assumed that they were identical, and that the *Sefer Yetzirah* mentioned by the Talmud is the *Sefer Yetzirah* required in the manufacture of a Golem.

The *Sefer Yetzirah* is traditionally ascribed to Abraham the Patriarch, although some kabbalists claimed its author was Rabbi Akiba. Gershom Scholem has dated the book between the third and the sixth century, and ascribes its authorship to an anonymous Palestinian scholar. A short work, less than two thousand words in length, the *Sefer Yetzirah* has inspired a plethora of commentary. Philosophers as well as mystics wrote commentaries to this work. The central subjects of the treatise — cosmology and cosmogony — were of great concern both to the medieval Jewish philosophers and to the medieval Jewish mystics. Though initially meant to be a speculative work, the *Sefer Yetzirah* was later considered by Jewish mystics to be a manual to be used for the act of creation itself. From being a book *about* creation, the *Sefer Yetzirah* became a book *of* creation. Originally understood by the mystics as a work of *kabbalah iyyunit* (mystical speculation), it later came to be utilized as a work of *kabbalah ma'asit* (practical mysticism). Rashi's observation indicates that by his time (i.e., eleventh century France), the *Sefer Yetzirah* was already understood to be a manual of magic. This tradition may predate Rashi as one may assume that he is reporting an already well-established tradition.

What is relevant to our discussion is that the *Sefer Yetzirah* describes the twenty-two letters of the Hebrew alphabet as being the foundation of creation. Through various combinations of the letters of the Hebrew alphabet, creation occurs. According to the *Sefer Yetzirah*, all twenty-two Hebrew letters derive from one name; i.e., from the Tetragrammaton, the ineffable four-letter name of God. The *Sefer Yetzirah* states:

> Twenty-two letter elements: He outlined them, hewed them out, weighted them, combined them, and exchanged them (i.e., He transformed them in accordance with certain laws), and through them (He) created the whole of all creation and everything else that would ever be created . . . it comes about that all creation and all language issue from one name (*Sefer Yetzirah* 2:2,5).

The notion that God creates the world by means of language – through words – is biblical. The idea that human beings can share in God's creative power by mastering formulae that combine and permutate letters of the alphabet is rabbinic in origin (see, e.g., *Berachot* 55a), but is considerably expanded by the medieval Jewish mystics.

For some Jewish mystics, letter permutations were used in the process of attaining the mystical experience (e.g., Abraham Abulafia). For other Jewish mystics, mastering the art of letter permutation and combination granted one the ability to create life itself. Rashi's comment regarding the ability of the talmudic rabbis to create both a calf and a man by letter combinations of the Name, reflects this notion. By a process of combining and permutating the letters of God's ineffable Name, creation can take place. Since the letters of the alphabet were the building blocks of creation, knowing how to manipulate those letters gives one access to the same forces that brought the world into being.

Rashi's terse commentary to the talmudic text under consideration introduces two elements that play an essential role in the development of the Golem legend: (1) the use of the *Sefer Yetzirah* not simply as a work about cosmology but as a tool to be used in the creative enterprise; (2) the idea that language is pregnant with creative potency, that language has the power to create worlds as well as words.

To this point, we have discussed Rabbah's creation of the first humanly created Golem. The text continues by telling us that Rabbah sent this "man" to Rabbi Zera. When Rabbi Zera spoke to the "man" he received no reply and from this he deduced that no ordinary person stood before him. Why did Rabbi Zera come to this conclusion?

What Rabbi Zera said to the "man" is equally enigmatic, "You are from the companions. Return to your dust."

The commentaries point out that when the "man" refused to respond, Rabbi Zera discerned that he was unable to speak (Rashi). Since the ability to speak is unique to human beings who embody the human soul (as distinct from the animal soul), Rabbi Zera concluded that the person who stood before him was not human, but was from the companions, i.e., from those scholars who are involved with the *Sefer Yetzirah* (commentary of Rabbi Samuel Edels – "Maharshah"). In addition, the Aramaic word translated literally

6

as "the companions," may also be translated as "the magical charmers," or simply as "magicians."

The term *ha-medaber* — the one who speaks — became a common designation for "human being" in medieval philosophical Hebrew. That the "man" who stood before Rabbi Zera failed to reply was taken by Rabbi Zera, as well as by medieval commentaries, as an indication that he was not truly human (see e.g. Nachmanides to Genesis 2:7).

Rabbi Zera's statement: Return to your dust, was taken to mean that the "man" disintegrated at Rabbi Zera's command. As we shall see, the legal and moral implications of Rabbi Zera's act were discussed in an eighteenth century responsum. At this point, however, one can identify two elements that are continuously found in subsequent versions of the Golem legend: (1) the Golem is human in all respects except one. The Golem lacks one vital characteristic that voids its claim to being human. In this text, that characteristic is the power of speech. As was mentioned, the commentaries interpreted the lack of speech as being indicative of the absence of a human soul. The Golem is a soulless, but not a life-less, human being. (2) Rabbi Zera's command indicates that language has the power to destroy as well as to create. (An interesting parallel to the text under discussion is found in Christian literature. A Christian legend tells that Albertus Magnus created a servant to help him. When Thomas Aquinas saw this servant, Thomas destroyed the servant as the work of the Devil.)

The description of a Golem as a soul-less human being is talmudic in origin. In a talmudic text in which the term "Golem" is used, the story of the creation of Adam is recounted. Unlike the previously discussed text that describes the Golem as a human creation, here the Golem is described as a creation of God. By creating a Golem, the human being reflects not only God's general creative ability but His specific ability to create a Golem. Described in this text as a "primitive" form of human being, as a soul-less

7

human being, the Golem represents the human creature in an incompleted primordial state. In a sense, the human creator of the Golem confronts the human creature – himself – in his own primitive, underdeveloped and primordial form. The human creator of the Golem confronts the human being – himself – as he once was, as he might have remained, as pure matter devoid of form, as a soul-less creature devoid of life and purpose. This notion may be echoed in the use of the term "Golem" in medieval philosophical Hebrew to denote matter without form, substance without purpose.

The text reads:

> Rabbi Johanan ben Hanina said: The (sixth day of creation) consisted of twelve hours. In the first hour his (i.e., Adam's) dust was gathered; in the second it (i.e., the dust) was made into a shapeless mass (Hebrew: *golem*); in the third his limbs were extended; in the fourth a soul was infused into him; in the fifth he arose and stood on his feet; in the sixth he gave (the animals) their names . . . (*Sanhedrin* 38b).

In various midrashic variants of this text, the sequence is reported differently. In the first hour God conceives of creating man; in the second He takes counsel with the angels regarding whether He should create man; in the third He assembles the dust; in the fourth He kneads the dust; in the fifth He shapes the form; in the sixth he makes him into a Golem; in the seventh He breathes a soul into him, etc. (see *Leviticus Rabbah* 29:1, *Tanhuma*, "Shmini" ¶8; compare other variants as *Midrash on Psalms* 92:3, *Pirke de Rabbi Eliezer* Ch. 11, *Avot d'Rabbi Natan*, Ch. 1, see also *Pesikta Rabbati* 46:2). In these versions, unlike the talmudic version, the Golem already has a human form, i.e., Adam's form. In these texts, the Golem is not a formless mass, but a manikin; human in form but not in essence. Thus, these

8

texts describe the state of "Golem" as soul-less, but *with* human form. Other midrashim reaffirm this description of Adam in his golemic stage, but they provide additional information regarding the Golem's activities in this state of suspended animation. For example, a midrash reads:

> "And He breathed into his nostrils" (Genesis 2:7). This teaches that He set him up as a Golem reaching from earth to heaven and then infused a soul into him (*Genesis Rabbah* 14:8).

From this text it is apparent that not only the ensouled primordial Adam (i.e., Adam before he sinned), but also Adam as Golem is described as a being of gigantic physical proportions. This motif surfaces in very late versions of the Golem legend where the Golem is described as being capable of assuming huge physical dimensions.

The term "Golem" means an "unformed mass." A form of the word "Golem" appears only once in the Bible (Psalm 139:16): "Your eyes saw my unformed mass (*galmi*), it was all recorded in Your book." A midrash interprets the verse as Adam saying to God: Your eyes saw my Golem. Furthermore, the phrase, "it was all recorded in Your book," is related by the midrash to the creation of Adam because, according to tradition, Adam is created on the Jewish New Year when God assesses the record of human deeds written in His "book" (see *Leviticus Rabbah* 29:1 where it is recorded that God decided and began to create Adam on New Year's Day).

A midrash reads:

> Rabbi Tanhuma in Rabbi Banaya's name and Rabbi Berekiah in Rabbi Eliezer's name said: He created him a Golem and he lay stretching from one end of the world to the other, as it is written, Your eyes saw my Golem. Rabbi Judah ben Simon said: While Adam lay as a Golem before Him who spoke and the world came into being, He showed him every generation and its sages,

every generation and its scribes, interpreters and leaders. Said He to him: Your eyes saw My Golem (i.e., the eyes of the Golem have seen My unformed world); the unformed substance (i.e., the Golem's potential descendants) which your eyes have seen is already written in the book of Adam — (as it is written) "This is the book of the generations of Adam" (Genesis 5:1). (*Genesis Rabbah* 24:2; Compare *Exodus Rabbah* 40:3; also see *Midrash on Psalms* 139:6, *Yalkut Shimoni* "Psalms" ¶887).

It may be that this midrash is trying to tell us that we are not only the descendants of Adam, but the descendants of a Golem as well. Perhaps, as the biblical verse indicates (Ps. 139:16), God saw Adam as Golem. In other words, God sees Adam — the human being — as essentially a Golem who becomes human only when realizing his/her potential symbolized in the text as the potential offspring of Adam-Golem. Otherwise, why would God show Adam his potential while still in golemic form rather than in his completed form?

The idea that a human being in a state of unfulfilled potentiality may be compared to a Golem is also found in a talmudic text. Regretfully, this text demonstrates the male chauvinism rather than the wisdom of the rabbis:

Rabbi Samuel ben Unya said in the name of Rab: A woman (before marriage) is a Golem, and concludes a covenant only with him who transforms her (into) a (useful) vessel, as it is written, "For your maker is your husband; the Lord of Hosts is His name" (Isaiah 54:5) (*Sanhedrin* 22b).

In his commentary to the term "Golem" in this text, Rashi comments, "Golem — a vessel that is not complete is called Golem."(Rashi's observation is based upon *Kelim* 12:6.)

In his *Commentary to the Mishnah*, Maimonides also in-

the moral novice. For them, the use of technical skills assumed the prior mastery of ethical insight.

The literature of the German Hasidim tells us not only *that* Golems were created, but also *how* Golems were created. Simply put, the ritual proceeded as follows.

Two or three adepts join together to create the Golem. The apparent limitation of the participants to two or three may reflect the mishnaic prohibition limiting speculation into the *ma'aseh bereshit* – the Workings of Creation. The designation of two *or* three may reflect the ambiguity of the mishnah (*Hagiga* 2:1) as to whether speculation into the "Workings of Creation" (*ma'aseh bereshit*) is limited to two (master and disciple) or to three (master and two disciples).

A magical circle is drawn to circumscribe the space in which the Golem is to be created. Virgin soil, taken from a mountain, is kneaded in running water. From this, the form of the Golem is made. Over this form various combinations of the letters of the Hebrew alphabet are recited. The formulae for these combinations derive from the *Sefer Yetzirah*. The recitations of these letter combinations animate the Golem, limb by limb. In some rituals, the formulae are recited while walking around the circle. Reciting these permutations in reverse order can serve to deactiviate the Golem and to transform him back into inert matter. For example, in pseudo-Saadya's commentary to the *Sefer Yetzirah* (2:5) that may have been available to the German Hasidim, the following statement appears, "I heard that Ibn Ezra created a creature in the presence of Rabbenu Tam (Rashi's grandson), and he said: See what God has put into the holy letters. And he (Tam) said: Turn backward (i.e., recite the letters backwards), and it returned to its original state."

The description of the ritual for the creation of a Golem by Eleazar of Worms – one of the leading personalities of German Hasidism – indicates that separate letter permutations are required for the creation of a female Golem from those required for the creation of a male Golem. The idea that a Golem may be female as well as male is found in a number of sources. Most noteworthy in this regard is a legend regarding the eleventh century poet and philosopher, Solomon ibn Gabirol.

Because he was afflicted by a severe skin disease, Ibn Gabirol lived in isolation. He therefore created a woman to keep house for him. When what he did became known, Gabirol was reported to the authorities. Because it was assumed that he had created her by magic, possibly for lewd activities, Gabirol was ordered to dismantle her. He did so, reducing her to the wood and hinges from which she was created.

That a female Golem was created is not unique in the Jewish literature about the Golem. What is unique is that Gabirol's Golem was not made of earth but of wood and hinges. Here one finds the roots of the portrayal of the Golem as a mechanical being, as an automaton, as a robot. This theme, as we shall see, is central to modern speculation about the moral and scientific implications of the Golem legend.

Gabirol's Golem is created for a specific purpose, i.e., to be a servant or perhaps to be a mistress. The Golem is created as a means to an end rather than as an end in itself. The issue of *why* the Golem is created, for what purpose is the Golem brought into being, becomes a central concern in the late medieval period. For the German Hasidim, however, the creation of the Golem is an end in itself. The Golem is created only to demonstrate the abilities of the one who created it. The Golem is created as part of an initiation ritual that culminates in mystical ecstasy. Consequently, the fate of the Golem after its creation, the function of the Golem after it has been brought into being, is of little concern for the German Hasidim.

Apparently with the sixteenth century, the post-creation career of the Golem begins to command attention. Here, as in the legend about Gabirol, the Golem is described functioning as a servant and perhaps also as a bodyguard for its creator and for his family. In later legends, the Golem is described as a being of immense physical strength, capable of assuming huge physical proportions (a throwback to the earlier midrashim [?]) who protects the Jews from physical abuse, from pogroms and from oppression. In other late sources, the Golem functions as a kind of spy. His gruff appearance permits him to infiltrate the gentile community where his task is to uncover plots against the Jews.

In the seventeenth century a new feature becomes part of the Golem-legend. Here the Golem is depicted as a creature which is potentially a danger to its creator. Both in Jewish and non-Jewish lore on the Golem this new dimension appears in tales of the alleged Golem making activities of the sixteenth century Rabbi Elijah of Helm (d. 1583). According to these legends this master of "practical kabbalah" created a Golem with a magical name on its forehead. In some variants the name is the Tetragrammaton; in others, the name is *Emet* – Truth – which, according to the Talmud, is the seal of God (*Sabbath* 55a). In some variants the name is inscribed into the forehead of the Golem; in other variants, the name is written on parchment and is attached to the Golem's forehead. (The midrash *Pirke de Rabbi Eliezer;* Chapter Four, notes that the Tetragrammaton is written on God's own forehead. This text appears to be the source for the statement in the *Hymn of Glory – Shir Ha-Kavod,* "The glory of His Holy Name is inscribed on His forehead.") When the Golem spontaneously grows to monumental physical proportions, Rabbi Elijah fears that its power might run amok and wreak havoc and destruction. To eliminate this threat, the rabbi reaches up and removes the parchment from the Golem's head thereby causing it to revert to dirt. When the Golem collapses, he injures the rabbi. In later versions of the legend, the Golem actually goes on a rampage of destruction before he is destroyed.

According to a version of the legend of Rabbi Elijah of

Helm, the rabbi deactivates the Golem by reaching up to erase the letter *alef* from the word *emet* that is inscribed on its forehead. By erasing the *alef* in the word for "truth" — *emet* — the word *met* — "dead" — remains.

That the Golem is brought to life by writing the word *emet* on its forehead is a notion that substantially predates Rabbi Elijah of Helm. According to a number of texts that derive from the literature of the German Hasidim of the thirteenth century which may reflect earlier traditions, God created Adam and inscribed the word *emet* on his forehead. When God wished to let Adam die, He removed the *alef* from *emet* and Adam became *met,* dead. Similarly, these texts relate, a Golem may be animated by writing *emet* on its forehead, and it may be destroyed by erasing the letter *alef.*

According to a text that Scholem dates in the early thirteenth century, the prophet Jeremiah and his son Sira created a Golem. After studying the *Sefer Yetzirah* for three years, they undertake the creation of a Golem. Through the use of letter permutations and combinations, they create a Golem. On its forehead they write the phrase, "the Lord God is Truth (*emet*)." But, once the Golem becomes vital, he takes the knife with which Jeremiah carved these words on its forehead and he scratches out the letter *alef.* Now the phrase reads, "the Lord God is dead." Jeremiah then asks the Golem why he did what he did. The Golem replies with a long parable. The message of the parable is that once human beings become creators they are in danger of forgetting the Creator. Once the creature becomes a creator overwhelmed by his own achievements he may act as if God is dead and he is now God. "What solution is there?" Jeremiah asks of the Golem. The Golem advises Jeremiah to destroy him by reversing the letter combinations used to create him. Jeremiah does so and the Golem returns to the elements.

While the legends about Rabbi Elijah and the Golem remind us of the physical danger with which the Golem's creation may threaten us, this text also depicts the spiritual danger which the Golem's creation holds forth for us. Jeremiah's wise and articulate Golem describes in his parable the danger of hubris when the human creature becomes a god-like creator.

While the human being is encouraged to develop his/her creative potentialities, he/she is also warned that there are dangers inherent in the creative endeavor, dangers to the physical, moral and spiritual well-being of the human creature-creator. One such medieval warning tells that the biblical character Enosh learned that God had created Adam from the earth. Enosh then took some earth, kneaded it into a human form and blew into its nostrils to animate it as God had given Adam life. Satan then slipped into the figure and gave it the appearance of life. Enosh and his generation worshipped the figure and, hence, idolatry began. The figure was worshipped instead of God. The product of human hubris and demonic ruse replaced God as an object of human adoration.

In the eighteenth century many of the motifs found in earlier versions of the Golem legend coalesced around the figure of Judah Loew, the Maharal of Prague. Known both in Jewish and Bohemian legend as a master of practical kabbalah, known from his writings as a master of kabbalistic theology, this sixteenth century scholar served as a perfect candidate upon whom to project the legends of the Golem. Ironically, none of the original legends about Judah Loew dating from the sixteenth or seventeenth centuries describe him as a creator of a Golem. Nowhere in his voluminous writings is there any hint of a preoccupation with the creation of a Golem. Nevertheless, beginning in the eighteenth century, Judah Loew of Prague was designated the central place in the Golem legend. Subsequent versions of and reflections upon the Golem legend centered upon *his* Golem.

Though Loew did not preoccupy himself with the creation of Golems, he does, as we have seen, comment on the talmudic reference to Rabbah's Golem. In *Hiddushei Aggadot* (on *Sanhedrin* 65b), he describes mystical adhesion to God as a necessary prerequisite for the creation of a Golem. In this commentary he also observes that the creation of a Golem with all human characteristics, e.g., speech, is beyond the realm of possibility: "For he (Rabbah) was a human being himself; and how would it then be possible for him to create a complete person like himself? Just as it is impossible to conceive that God, who is supreme over everything, would create one like Himself." Furthermore, according to Loew, meditation on the divine Names contained in the *Sefer Yetzirah* is like any other kind of prayer, "because (in prayer) one calls (upon God) . . . Therefore, the *Sefer Yetzirah,* in which is recorded the divine Names by which God created the world . . . is not outside of nature . . . How can one claim that pronunciation of the Names by which the world came into being is outside the natural order?" (*Be'er Ha-Golah* Ch. 2).

In the most popular version of the legend of Loew's Golem, Judah Loew creates a Golem either to be his servant or to protect the Jews from pogroms. One Sabbath eve, the Golem runs amok, ripping up the Jewish ghetto of Prague. Loew then destroys the Golem by removing the magical name that gave it life. Loew places the dust of the Golem's remains in the attic of the Altneuschul synagogue in Prague. He decrees that in the future no one is permitted to ever ascend to the attic to view the Golem's remains.

Rabbi Zevi Ashkenazi was the grandson of Elijah of Helm. He also was related to Judah Loew of Prague. In a curious responsum, Ashkenazi raises the question of whether a Golem may be included in a quorum for prayer, a *minyan*. The complete text of the responsum follows in English translation:

> I became doubtful (concerning the resolution of
> the following question): Is (the case of) a man,

created (by means of magically employing) the *Sefer Yetzirah* identical (to the case) reported in the *Tractate Sanhedrin*?

Namely, "Rabbah created a man (and sent him to Rabbi Zera. Rabbi Zera spoke to him but received no answer. Thereupon he said to him — You and a creature of magicians. Return to your dust" *San.* 65b). So it has also been asserted concerning my grandfather, the Gaon, our Master and Teacher, Rabbi Elijah, chief rabbi of the Holy Community of Helm. Who is allowed to be counted as one of ten (i.e., a quorum for prayer) in matters which require ten, i.e., (recitation of prayers as) *Kaddish, Kedushah,* for it is written, "I (God) will be sanctified amidst Israel"? Do we include (such an individual as the artificially created man) or do we say that since it is taught in *Sanhedrin*, "He who raises an orphan in his home, Scripture ascribes it to him as though he had begotten him? For it is written, 'Five sons of Michal, the daughter of Saul whom she bore to Adriel' (II Samuel 21:8). 'Did not Merab bear them? Yes, but Michal raised them (and they are therefore called her sons)" (*Sanhedrin* 19a). In the present case as well (the artificially created man is considered a child of the one who created him; therefore a regular human being; therefore he can be counted).

Since the workings of the hands of the righteous is involved, he is to be included for the works of the hands of the righteous are their progeny. (See Rashi to Genesis 6:9 based on *Genesis Rabbah* 30:6). (So far, he is included.)

But it seems to me that as a result of meeting Rabbi Zera who said: "You are the work of magicians, return to your dust," he was killed. And don't you think that if there would have been a need to include him amongst a quorum that Rabbi Zera would have "cast him from the world"?

(It thus appears that) there is no prohibition of murder concerning him. (Otherwise Rabbi Zera would be guilty of murder.) For Scripture remarks – and I know there are other possible explanations: "Whosoever sheds a *man*'s blood, by man shall his blood be shed (for in the image of God made He man." Genesis 9:5). (That is to say,) only a *man* formed within a human being; that is, only (killing one who was) a fetus formed within his mother's womb (is counted as murder). Nevertheless, since he (the artificially created man) has a purpose, he (Rabbi Zera) should not have cast him out of existence. But it is certain that he (the artificially created man) is not counted amongst the ten needed for holy deeds (*Responsa of Haham Zvi Ashkenazi*, No. 93).

This responsum can serve as a transitionary point between discussion of the classical origins and the contemporary implications of the Golem legend. This text reiterates a number of issues raised by earlier Jewish literature about the Golem while it anticipates a variety of contemporary implications of the Golem legend.

This responsum is curious in that it is not a responsum at all. A responsum is a legal opinion offered by a rabbi in response to a question put to him. This "responsum" is a discussion of a problem the author put to himself.

That Ashkenazi raises the question of whether a Golem may help form a *minyan*, and that he and others treat it as a viable halakhic issue demonstrates the seriousness with which the Golem was taken. In addition, it should be noted that Ashkenazi's son, the eminent and controversial Rabbi Jacob Emden, also discusses the issue of counting the Golem in the *minyan*. In one of his responsa   (*Sheelat*

Yaavetz II, no. 82), Emden concludes that since a minor or an imbecile cannot be counted in a quorum for prayer, it goes without saying that a senseless Golem cannot be counted. Incidentally, it is from Emden's halakhic, kabbalistic, and autobiographical writings that we learn the details of the story of Rabbi Elijah of Helm and his Golem (see, e.g. his autobiography, *Megilat Sefer*, beginning).

Though Ashkenazi addresses the particular question of whether a Golem can be included in a *minyan*, he also implicitly raises a general question that becomes pertinent to a discussion of contemporary implications of the Golem legend.

Every legal system contains a notion of "persons in the law." A "person" is one with rights and duties, with privileges and obligations. In a sense, Ashkenazi raises the implicit question of whether "artificially" created entities can be "persons in the law," having privileges and duties under the law. By excluding the Golem from the *minyan*, Ashkenazi articulates the position that "artificial" individuals do not qualify to be considered legal persons. The implications of this view will be discussed below.

Finally, Ashkenazi examines the question of whether Rabbi Zera was guilty of murder for destroying the "man" artificially created by Rabbah. He concludes that since the "man" was not human, destroying him could not be murder. Nevertheless, Rabbi Zera's action may not be justifiable. The Golem may have been devoid of a human soul, but it was not devoid of life. Killing it may not have been murder, but it was an act of killing nonetheless. If the Golem is considered inert matter, however, then it cannot be considered alive. Therefore, destroying it might be classified as a tort, a destruction of property, but it is not a criminal act of murder. This observation as well will become pertinent to the discussion below regarding the status of "artificially" created beings and to the question of our responsibility, if any, toward them.

From this survey of the classical literature regarding the Golem one may distill a number of observations that become relevant to a discussion of some of the contemporary implications of the Golem legend:

1. The creation of "artificial" beings is sanctioned and even encouraged by classical Jewish literature.

2. As a creator, the human being is most human. Through creativity, the human being expresses his/her godlike qualities. Human creativity articulates *imitatio dei*.

3. Creativity expresses an attribute that we derive from God and that we share with God. Therefore, creativity can be a means of achieving communion with God. Human creativity can provide an entre to an intense religious or even mystical experience.

4. Creativity is a double-edge sword. The creative endeavor is replete with dangers.

5. That which we create to help insure our physical comfort or our physical security may ultimately threaten our physical comfort and/or our physical security. The creative act, by its nature, creates the potential for self-harm and for self-destruction.

6. Creativity can provide psychological fulfillment, but it can also become psychologically self-destructive. Once the creature becomes a creator, the creature may begin to think of him/herself exclusively as a creator. One may have delusions of grandeur and omnipotence.

7. Creativity can be an entre to spiritual rapture, but it can also be an invitation to idolatry. One may begin to worship and to adorate what one creates, thus becoming subservient to one's own creation. Once this occurs, the human creator-creature may begin to measure him/ herself against that which has been created.

8. Creativity may begin as an act of faith in God, the source of all creativity. But, it may develop into a negation of faith, a rejection of God. Impressed by his/her own creations, the individual may replace worship of God with self-worship. Technological achievement, man-made miracles,

may lead one to the illusion of human self-sufficiency, to the conclusion that belief in God is unnecessary. Technological advance threatens to lead us to the conclusion that "God is dead."

9. With the creation of "artificial" beings, a whole new set of moral problems comes into being. With the creation of such beings, the nature of the relationship between creator and creature must be addressed. The question of the purpose of the existence of the artificial being must be justified. The legal status of the being and the responsibility of and for the being's actions must be clarified.

10. Moral prerequisites are required of one undertaking the creation of artificial beings. Ethical safeguards and controls must be built-in to the process of the creation and manipulation of life.

11. A creature reflects back upon its creator. Human beings reflect back upon God. Golems reflect back upon human beings. Reflection upon the nature of the things we create can serve as a conduit to self-reflection, to self-understanding.

12. Adam was the first Golem. Adam is a Golem who became human. Is the converse also possible: can a human become a Golem?

In considering the contemporary implications of the Golem legend, our discussion must be tentative and suggestive, rather than definitive. The questions raised are still being formulated. The answers exceed our present grasp. Yet, what is clear is the pertinence of this classical legend for our times, and for future times.

Once a product of fantasy and of imagination, the Golem legend – its implications, its observations – is a matter of urgent relevance. The questions it engenders and the issues it evokes are matters of crushing contemporary concern. We shall now proceed to examine some of these questions, some of these implications.

As was mentioned above, Ashkenazi's responsum can serve as a link between the classical legend and the contemporary implications of that legend. Ashkenazi's responsum raises the following questions:

What is the legal status of a Golem? Is a Golem a person? Can a Golem be considered as someone's property? Can a Golem be human? Can a human be a Golem? Is destroying a Golem murder? Can a Golem be intelligent? Is an "intelligent" Golem different from other Golems? In dealing with the contemporary implications of the Golem legend, these questions must be addressed.

The question of whether an artificially created living being can be considered someone's property has been dealt with by the American judicial system. In a fascinating case that was finally decided by the United States Supreme Court, the issue of the ownership of an artificially created new life-form was discussed (*Diamond* vs. *Chakrabarty*, June 1980). Ananda M. Chakrabarty is a microbiologist who created a "human-made genetically engineered bacterium capable of breaking down multiple components of crude oil." In other words, Dr. Chakrabarty created a new bacterium capable of "eating" oil slicks. He applied for a patent for the new bacterium. The U.S. Patent Office denied him a patent on the grounds that micro-organisms are "products of nature" and that as living things they are not patentable subject matter. Chakrabarty brought suit against the U.S. Commissioner of Patents and Trademarks, Sidney Diamond, claiming that the new organism is indeed patentable. The case went up to the U.S. Supreme Court and the Court, by a five to four vote, affirmed Chakrabarty's position. This case established a precedent. It affirmed the right of an individual to own an artificially created being. What the Court did not establish, however, are the liabilities and responsibilities of the creator of artificial beings for their activities.

The issue of ownership of and responsibility for artificially created beings becomes especially poignant when it relates to life-saving or life-destroying organisms. For example, would the creator (or the company sponsoring the creation) of an organism that "escapes" a laboratory and kills animals, crops or people be liable for such damage? Could a creator (or a company sponsoring the creation) of an organism that cheaply mass produces rare and expensive life-saving drugs be required to offer such drugs for reasonable prices, with a reasonable profit margin? These kinds of questions remain to be addressed and resolved in civil law. Because the sources regarding the Golem legend do not discuss the question of the liability of the creator of a Golem, there is neither precedent nor guidance forthcoming from the classical literature of the Golem legend on this matter.

Because the Supreme Court decision left many legal and moral questions unanswered, a group of American religious leaders wrote to President Carter in 1980 expressing their concern regarding the moral problems that the creation of artificial life raises. As a response to the articulation of this concern, a presidential commission was asked to investigate the social and ethical implications of genetic engineering. After two years of hearings and discussion, the Commission submitted an informative and elucidating report entitled *Splicing Life* (November 1982). In this report both the potential promise and the potential danger of genetic engineering with human beings is carefully discussed. In reviewing the possible dangers of genetic engineering, the report refers to the Golem legend:

> Like the tale of the Sorcerer's apprentice or the myth of the golem created from lifeless dust by the 16th century rabbi, Loew of Prague, the story of Dr. Frankenstein's monster serves as a reminder of the difficulty of restoring order if a creation intended to be helpful proves harmful instead. Indeed, each of these tales conveys a painful irony: in seeking to extend their control over the world, people may lessen it. The artifices they create to do their bidding may rebound destructively

against them – the slave may become the master.

Apprehension that the Golem-slave will become the master of its creator is not simply a concern of the Commission, nor is it merely a restatement of the master-slave dialectic developed by Hegel. That the Golem will enslave its master is a common theme in the literary "spin-offs" of the Golem legend. For example, in the Capek brothers' famous play, *R.U.R.* (Act 3), where the term "robot" is first coined, we read, "Mankind will never cope with the Robots, and will never have control over them. Mankind will be overwhelmed in the deluge of these dreadful living machines, will be their slave, will live at their mercy."

The report of the Presidential Commission notes a study done by the National Science Foundation which found that most Americans opposed most restrictions on scientific research in all areas but one – creation of new life-forms and genetic engineering with human beings. While the Commission concurred that there are valid reasons for this apprehension, it also asserted that much popular opposition to genetic engineering was based upon fear grounded in a lack of awareness of the nature of genetic engineering, and of the potential benefits it holds forth. While the Commission was sensitive to the possible moral abuses of genetic engineering, it also indicated that it might be unethical to stifle the potential benefits that genetic engineering may bring to many people. For example, drugs could be produced in large quantities at comparatively little cost that could help treat medical problems that otherwise would either not be treated, or that could be treated only at extraordinary cost. Already, gene splicing techniques have produced several useful human growth hormones that treat dwarfism. Drugs to fight diabetes, hemophilia and even cancer could be produced in great quantities through gene splicing techniques. In addition, gene splicing could be utilized to correct genetic defects both before and after birth that otherwise would have tragic or even fatal consequences. Finally, because of natural or man-induced climatic or other changes in our environment, genetic engineering may forestall extensive catastrophe. For example, if a sudden shift of climate were to occur, the use of genetic engineering to alter quickly the genetic composition of agricultural plants may save whole populations from mass starvation.

As was noted above, Judah Loew and others described the creation of artificial life by means of the *Sefer Yetzirah* as acting in consonance with the natural order of creation. In other words, such acts are essentially "natural" and do not represent a contravening of the natural order. Similarly, the Commission observed that gene splicing occurs naturally within bacteria. Therefore, it concluded that "the basic processes underlying genetic engineering are thus *natural* and not revolutionary. Indeed, it was the discovery that these processes were (naturally) occurring that suggested to scientists the great possibilities and basic methods of gene splicing. What is new, however, is the ability of scientists to control the processes."

Fear that artificially created organisms might endanger human life was found by the Commission to be a largely unfounded fear, grounded in the public's lack of knowledge regarding the controls under which such activities were conducted. It found both scientific and government controls upon such experimentation to be more than adequate. Professor Seymour Siegel, an eminent Jewish theologian who was a member of the Commission, reported the following in an address to the Rabbinical Assembly (*Proceedings* 1978):

> The National Institute of Health has formulated guidelines to be followed by laboratories sponsoring DNA research. These guidelines have reduced the danger of these experiments to practically zero . . . I can testify personally, as a member of the Biohazards Committee of the giant pharmaceutical firm, Hoffman-LaRoche, as to the exquisite care which is taken in the pro-

tection of the environment and the reseachers involved in DNA experiments. . . . Thus it seems obvious to me that the potentially great benefits to mankind in carrying on these researches far outweigh any possible harm.

Though the Commission felt that genetic engineering is adequately monitored in the United States, it nevertheless recommended that such careful monitoring continue. It also reinforced a popular apprehension regarding the dangers of genetic engineering in a non-democratic political setting, or for use in developing pathogenic micro-organisms for biological warfare or for terrorism (see e.g., Frank Herbert's novel, *The White Plague*). Furthermore, the Commission warned that the hubris of the scientist that might lead him or her to create artificial beings without regard to the potential physical and moral dangers of such action had to be controlled. It denounced as outrightly unethical certain possible uses of genetic engineering such as the creation of a genetically engineered slave population of partly human and partly animal beings. In short, the Commission in general, and the theologians on the Commission in particular, felt that in itself genetic engineering is good, that it articulates the biblical view that human beings are cocreators with the Supreme Creator. However, it also maintained that genetic engineering, like any human activity, can express itself as a misuse of human freedom with concomitant harmful results. As in much of Jewish literature regarding the Golem, the Commission concluded that the creation of artificial life should be permitted, and even encouraged. However, such activities must be done with expert care and with a keen awareness of the potentially harmful consequences of such actions (see for example, John Saul's novel, *The God Project*, and Michael Crichton's novel, *The Andromeda Strain*).

One of the issues touched, but not elaborated upon by the Commission, was the development of new techniques in the treatment of barren couples, e.g., "test-tube babies." Such techniques almost seem to have been anticipated by Ashkenazi's responsum.

In Shakespeare's *Macbeth*, the witches predict that Macbeth could only be killed by one who was not of woman born (Act IV, Scene One; Act V, Scene Eight). Macduff, who was born by means of a Cesarean, fits into this category, and slays Macbeth. Macduff's status as a human being – despite the conditions of his birth – is never questioned. Nor would Ashkenazi question it. However, while Ashkenazi would not disenfranchise one born by other than "natural" means from the category of human beings, he does disqualify the Golem from enjoying human status because it was not "formed within his mother's womb."

When the first test-tube baby was born in England, the news media compared the test-tube baby to the Golem. Conceived "artificially," i.e., outside of the womb, the test-tube baby would be comparable to a Golem according to Ashkenazi's definition.

"Test-tube babies" or *in vitro* fertilization is only one of a number of techniques that may be utilized to bring about "artificial" conception. Nevertheless, all such methods of artificial conception have raised serious moral questions with which ethicians and theologians must deal. Among such techniques are artificial insemination, *in vitro* fertilization, artificial embryonization, parthenogenesis, and cloning. Some of these techniques are currently commonly practised. Others may or may not have occurred. Others may be beyond the abilities of current scientific technology.

Artificial insemination is widely practiced today in the United States. It has been estimated that more than a quarter of a million people have been conceived in this manner. As many as ten thousand to twenty-five thousand Americans each year may currently be conceived in this manner. Because of the confidentiality surrounding this procedure, exact numbers cannot be known.

Artificial insemination takes two forms: artificial

31

insemination-husband (AIH) and artificial insemination-donor (AID). While some have raised moral and religious questions regarding AIH, more have raised questions regarding AID, e.g., is AID adultery, could a child conceived by AID potentially marry his/her own half-brother or half-sister, etc.? Surprisingly, a leading halakhic authority, Rabbi Moses Feinstein, ruled that AID cannot be considered adultery since no physical act of copulation is involved, and because no intention to commit adultery is present in the mind of the woman involved. However, Feinstein's position is not accepted by many halakhic authorities, e.g., Eliezer Waldenberg, Immanual Jakobovitz, and Isaac Klein. (For a review of the literature, see, Fred Rosner, "Artificial Insemination in Jewish Law," *Judaism* (Fall 1970) 19:4, pp. 452-465.) In American law, too, there has been much discussion on this issue. For example, what are the rights and obligations of the husband of a woman who conceives and who delivers a child by means of AID? If, for example, the couple divorces, does the husband have obligations to support the child, or, on the other hand, does he have rights to custody of the child?

In many states, the law presumes that a child born within a marriage is the natural child of the couple. This, however, is not true in all states. In addition, where there is evidence that the child is not the natural child of the husband, as in a case of AID, the father's claim to the child, for instance in a custody suit, would be weakened. Therefore, in a number of states, the husband of a wife who has delivered a child conceived by means of AID may be counselled by an attorney to adopt the child.

In recent years the practice of "surrogate mothers" has become increasingly common. In this situation, a barren woman married to a fertile man agrees to an arrangement whereby a child is born who is the natural child of the husband. A woman volunteer is impregnated through artificial insemination with the sperm of the husband. When the child is born, the natural mother releases her rights to the child. The natural father acknowledges his paternity of the child. The father's wife then adopts the child as her own.

In *in vitro* fertilization, an ovum is removed from a woman. Such women usually are unable to conceive children naturally because of some reproductive malfunction, usually in their Fallopian tubes. The ovum is then fertilized in a petri dish from the sperm of a man. In the United States there are strict guidelines on *in vitro* fertilization, and, therefore, to date, only married people have been involved with this procedure. If conception occurs and if gestation begins normally, the fetus is then placed into the uterus, where, it is hoped, it will become implanted, and a natural gestation will occur to term, i.e., to birth.

Artificial embryonization is a comparatively new procedure. Successfully used in animals, it may become a common medical procedure on humans very soon. Artificial embryonization is somewhat like the opposite of donor insemination. Here, an ovum is taken from a female volunteer. It is then fertilized by a male, usually *in vitro* as in the case of a test-tube baby. Or, the egg could be implanted in his wife's womb where it could be fertilized *in vivo*. The child would genetically be the father's but not the mother's. The woman giving birth to the child would be its natural mother, but not its genetic mother.

In parthenogenesis, an ovum would be stimulated to gestate either chemically or electrically. The child would always be female and would carry only the mother's chromosomes. No fertilization would occur. No sperm is involved. While parthenogenesis has been accomplished with animals, there is no evidence (though there is speculation) that is has been accomplished with humans.

In cloning, the nucleus of an ovum is replaced by a nucleus of a cell taken from the body of a person. After gestation has begun, the ovum is then planted in a womb. The resulting child would be genetically identical to the person from whose body the nucleus was taken. In this way, a person could genetically reproduce himself or herself. Genetically speaking one could become one's own parent/child. To date, there is no substantiated record of such a procedure having been done on humans, though cloning has been done on plants and animals. To date, cloning of humans is more a part of science fiction than science. (David Rorvik, in *In His Image: The Cloning of a Man* claims that a human child born in 1976 is a clone. Also see N. Freedman's novel *Joshua, Son of None*, and, Ira Levin's *The Boys From Brazil.*)

Orthodox Jewish halakhists and Roman Catholic moral theologians find many, if not all, of these procedures to be problematic. One serious objection that they make to procedures such as *in vitro* fertilization relates to the fate of fertilized eggs that are discarded. For example, if more than one ovum from a given woman is fertilized, only one may be implanted and the others destroyed. In some cases, one fertilized egg may be implanted while other fertilized eggs might be frozen for future use; for example, if the first spontaneously aborts, or if one is needed for a future pregnancy. Fertilized eggs that do not gestate normally might be frozen and subsequently be destroyed once a birth occurs.

In Australia, a case was reported of a woman who became a candidate for *in vitro* fertilization. Four eggs were removed and fertilized with her husband's sperm. Three were implanted while the fourth was frozen. Four months after fertilization, she miscarried, losing the three embryos. The fourth frozen embryo was thawed and successfully implanted. A normal birth is anticipated by her physicians (*Parade*, July 10, 1983, p. 12).

In a New York State court case (*Del Zio* vs. *Presbyterian Hospital*, 74 Civ. 3588, New York City), a woman sued and collected damages when her egg, fertilized *in vitro*, was destroyed in the laboratory. A fertilized egg might not gestate well, either *in vitro* or *in vivo.* In such a case, it may be destroyed. Assuming that life begins at conception, some theologians oppose processes such as *in vitro* because, in their view, ensouled fetuses are likely to be "killed."

Ashkenazi's responsum can provide a basis for an alternative position. Because he identifies "artificial" conception but not "artificial" birth as the essential characteristic of a Golem, one may assume that he would consider a fetus *conceived* by artificial means to be a Golem, and therefore not human, while he would consider an artificially conceived child *delivered* by vaginal or Caesarean means to be a normal human being. From such a perspective, a child conceived *in vitro* and delivered in birth would be a normal human being, but during the process of conception and gestation it would not necessarily fall under that category. Therefore, destroying such a fetus — as in the cases mentioned above — would not be considered murder. Hence, a primary objection to the use of methods that might prove the only means by which barren couples could have children, would be overcome.

In the case of surrogate motherhood the child is adopted by the wife of the natural father. In artificial embryonization, the birthing mother, in a very physical way, adopts the genetic child of the ovum donor by having that fertilized ovum introduced into her body for gestation and birth. Because this procedure is so new, the courts have produced no case law as to whether the genetic mother (i.e., the ovum donor) or the birthing mother is the legal mother of the child. Neither have the courts determined whether the ovum is the property of the donor who then would have certain rights vis-a-vis the ovum. Nor have the courts determined whether the "sale" of an ovum is a legally binding sale. In the absence of legal precedent on the matter, one may analogize the situation of artificial embryonization to an adopted child. The genes of the potential child are in a sense adopted by the birthing mother. Similarly, in the case of parthenogenesis a man may eventually become the adopting father of the child that results from the employment of this procedure.

The adoption analogy is utilized by Ashkenazi in his responsum. The Golem is compared to the adopted child of its creator. Though Ashkenazi eventually rejects this analogy, it may nevertheless be employed in the cases under consideration. To sum up: until birth, the fetus created "artificially" would have the status of Golem, and would not be considered human in all respects. However, at birth or at a stage of "viability" (i.e., the fetus could survive outside of the womb), the child would be considered the natural (i.e., the genetic) child of the parent providing his/her genes, and the adopted child of the other parent.

Legal discussion regarding the patentability and ownership of an artificially created being such as a microbe does not address the problem of the status of "higher" forms of being such as Golems, i.e., artificially created human beings. This question leads us back to Ashkenazi's problem of whether a Golem can be considered a "person" in the law, to the problem of whether the law should recognize such beings as "artificial persons" with the status of "natural persons" under the law, and to the problem of whether the Golem can be considered a "person" in any respect.

American law recognizes two categories of "persons": "natural" and "artificial." In American law a person is such, not because he or she is human but because rights and duties are ascribed to him or her or it. A natural person is an individual human being. An example of an artificial person would be a corporation or a county or an estate of a deceased individual. Thus, while Ashkenazi would not consider an artificial being as a legal person, American law readily allows for the creation of artificial legal persons (see *Black's Law Dictionary*, "Persons").

In many situations the wisdom of admitting artificial persons to the status of legal persons may be questioned. Ashkenazi's refusal to admit artificial entities to the status of legal personhood may be well advised. For example, a corporation by its very nature, would not be punishable in the same manner as would be a human being (i.e., imprisonment, capital punishment). For example, a corporation that releases carcinogenic wastes or poisonous industrial substances into a lake from which people draw their drinking water might only be liable for a nominal statutory fine, while a person causing deliberate harm to other persons in an identical manner might also be liable to imprisonment. The acceptance of artificial persons as legal persons might encourage individual officials of corporations to seek personal legal immunity by hiding behind a "corporate shield." Thus, there may be some wisdom to Ashkenazi's position that refuses to grant legal personhood to artificial beings.

As was noted above, Ashkenazi maintained that Rabbi Zera was not guilty of murder because the "man" artificially created by Rabbah was not human. Similarly, Ibn Gabirol destroyed the female Golem he had created by dismantling her mechanical parts by order of the court. However, what would be the case if she had been part human and part mechanical. Would his action have been an act of murder? This question has been raised in science fiction literature. For example, in his story, *Fires of Night*, Dennis Etchison asks whether killing a person with artificial limbs and/or organs would be murder. At what point would such an individual cross over the line from being a human to being a machine, a Golem? When would such an individual stop being a human who is part machine and become merely a machine that is part human? This question is amplified by Martin Caidin in his novel *Cyborg* which became the basis for the television program, "The Six Million Dollar Man." In this story, an American astronaut crash-lands. His destroyed limbs are replaced by bionic limbs. He is now literally half-human, half-machine. With the fast paced developments in bionics and the use of artificial organs, questions originally raised by science fiction writers currently fall under the domain of medical ethics.

The question of the legal status of individuals with artificial mechanical organs came to the fore with the first suc-
cessful implantation of an artificial heart into a human being in 1982. Great consternation was evoked when the
Ashkenazic chief rabbi of Israel, Shlomo Goren, declared
that a person with an artificial heart is no longer to be considered human and that killing him would not be murder.
Would such a situation be analogous to the case of Rabbi
Zera's destruction of Rabbah's Golem? Could Ashkenazi's
responsum serve as a precedent for Goren's position?

Goren's view cannot be analogized to that of Ashkenazi
because Rabbah's Golem was created artificially from the
elements while the artificial heart recipient's status was
human when the mechanical heart was implanted, and,
there is no reason to believe that he would lose this status
simply because of the implantation of an artificial organ or
limb, no matter how vital. To accept Goren's view and to
carry it to its logical extremes would mean to deny human
status to a patient on a heart-lung machine during surgery,
to a person with a cardiac pacemaker, to a kidney patient
on a dialysis machine during treatment, and perhaps even
to a diabetic whose survival is dependent upon certain kinds
of processed insulin. Surely, more than the introduction of
an artificial limb or organ is required to disenfranchise an
individual of his/her status as a human being. From the view
that a Golem is not a human, it does not follow that a human
can become a Golem, a non-human.

In his responsum on whether a Golem may be included
in a *minyan*, Ashkenazi's son, Jacob Emden, argues that a
Golem may not be included because it lacks intelligence.
Furthermore, as we have seen, Rabbi Zera was not deemed
guilty of murdering Rabbah's Golem — according to some
of the commentaries — because it lacked speech, and,
therefore, intelligence. Such an approach would deny a
Golem any rights and would make it liable to any possible

abuse.

An interesting observation on this issue is made by Isaiah Horowitz, the great sixteenth century kabbalist in his *magnum opus, Shnei Luhot Ha-Brit* ("va-yeshev," 3:30a).

According to the biblical text, Joseph was a tattletale who reported his brothers' wrongdoings to his father, Jacob (Genesis 37:3). According to the commentaries, one of the items Joseph reported was that his brothers were engaged in illicit sexual activities. Horowitz claims that such was the appearance, but not the reality.

According to Horowitz (who quotes the text from *Sanhedrin* regarding Rabbah's artificially created man), Joseph's brothers were not engaged sexually with human women, but with a female Golem.

Horowitz reports that Abraham wrote the *Sefer Yetzirah* and passed it down to his son, Isaac, who then passed it down to his son, Jacob. Jacob, in turn, passed it down to his sons, Joseph's brothers. Jacob's sons used the *Sefer Yetzirah* to create a female Golem with which they enjoyed sexual relations. But, since she was not human, these actions could not be considered sinful. Joseph, therefore, rendered an inaccurate report. Unlike Ibn Gabirol, the brothers were not required to destroy a female Golem created for sexual purposes. According to Horowitz, such sexual activity is not prohibited because the female Golem cannot be considered human.

Zevi Hirsch Shapira in his *Darkhei Teshuvah* (Jerusalem, 1967 – *Shulhan Arukh – Yoreh Deah* 7:11, p. 38) comments on Horowitz's discussion. According to Shapira, the female Golem lacked the powers of speech and intelligence, and, therefore, it should be excluded from the category of being human. But, what if the female Golem had intelligence? What if Rabbah's male Golem had intelligence? Would Jacob's sons have been guilty then of abusing her? Would Rabbi Zera have been guilty then of murder?

According to the medieval kabbalistic text, *Sefer Ha*

Bahir (para. no. 196), Rabbah's Golem did not have the power of speech because it was not created by the completely righteous (see Raba's statement). However, if it were so created, it would have had the power of speech and would have been intelligent. Therefore, the inability to create an intelligent Golem reflects a flaw in the creator of the Golem that becomes embodied in the Golem he creates. (Compare Judah Loew on *Sanhedrin* 65b where he denies the possibility of creating an intelligent, speaking Golem.)

The daring late hasidic master, Gershon Hanokh Leiner of Radzyn, in his controversial *Sidrei Taharot* (on *Ohalot*) goes even further than the *Sefer Ha Bahir*. Gershon Hanokh agrees that Rabbi Zera was justified in killing Rabbah's Golem because it lacked intelligence and consequently it is regarded "as an animal in human form and it is permissible to kill it." However, he adds, if an intelligent Golem had been created, "he would have the legal status of a true man . . . even as regards being counted in a *minyan* . . . and he would be the same as if God had created him." Thus, Gershon Hanokh admits the possibility of considering an artificially created being who manifests all normal human traits, including intelligence, as a human being. Gershon Hanokh would grant human personhood to such an "artificially" created human being. Destroying such a Golem, it would follow, would be murder. If Joseph's brothers had sexually abused such a female Golem, Gershon Hanokh would hold them liable for rape.

In making his claim that a Golem might be considered human, Gershon Hanokh articulates his disagreement with the position of Judah Loew of Prague and others who maintained that a Golem could never have all human characteristics, and, hence, could never be considered a human being. For Loew, and for others noted above, a human artifact could never be a human being. Gershon Hanokh's view is willing to eradicate any absolute distinction between humans and Golems. For Gershon Hanokh, a Golem that meets certain prerequisites can be considered human. Loew, on the other hand, insists upon a firm line of demarcation between humans and Golems. For Loew, a Golem by definition cannot be considered a human.

This clash of views between Loew and Gershon Hanokh finds contemporary expression in the vast literature on the question of whether machines that mainfest human traits can be considered human in any sense. If, for example, one considers intelligence to be the essential trait in determining whether one is human, could an intelligent machine then be considered human? Gershon Hanokh might answer in the affirmative, while Judah Loew would answer in the negative. Like Judah Loew, some contemporary philosophers and scientists maintain that a machine, even an intelligent machine, could not be considered human because it always would lack some essential human trait. Some thinkers of this school would further maintain that human intelligence like human nature is *sui generis* and that just as a machine must always be distinguished from a human being, so must machine intelligence or artificial intelligence be distinguished from human intelligence. Other thinkers of this school might argue, for example, that while intelligence is an essential human trait, nevertheless, the possession of intelligence by a non-human being, e.g., an extra-terrestrial or a dolphin, would not ipso facto qualify such a being for human status. Nor would the absence of a normal degree of human intelligence − e.g., an imbecile − disqualify a human person from the status of a human being.

Philosophers and theologians who refuse to grant human status and/or human intelligence to Golems and machines rest their argument upon a fundamental presupposition − the unique, *sui generis* nature of the human being. Where these thinkers may disagree is on the question of what is it that makes human existence *sui generis*, what quality is it that makes human beings human. Some maintain that

41

the very fact that each human being is different from each other human being is itself adequate evidence for affirming the unique nature not only of the human person, but of each and every human person (see e.g. *Sanhedrin* 37a, *Avot d'Rabbi Natan*, Ch. 31). Machines and Golems can be duplicated; human beings cannot. Others hold that ensoulment is what makes the human being unique. The Golem, by definition, is a soulless, though not necessarily a lifeless, being. Thus, to speak of a "human Golem" in this view would be a contradiction in terms, a linguistically meaningless statement. Still others hold that qualities such as the ability to laugh, to create, to be embarrassed, to express emotion, to love, to carry on a telephone conversation, to be self-conscious, to act freely and spontaneously, to have hopes and dreams, to be inconsistent and unpredictable, etc., are peculiarly human and cannot be found in machines. Furthermore, even if such paradigmatically "human" characteristics were apparently present in machines, such machines still would not qualify for human personhood, as such characteristics would merely represent a reflection of those characteristics of the designer of the machine. Following Judah Loew's thinking, just as the human person, though created in God's image, is not God, so a Golem or a machine into which certain human characteristics are programmed, would not be considered a human being. In their discussion of the question of "artificial intelligence," a number of contemporary philosophers have argued a similar view.

A number of philosophers have maintained that we tend to confuse the data programmed into a machine by a human being with intelligence. For example, as philosopher Michael Polanyi has observed, the thought that we detect in the working of a machine is properly speaking only the thought of the designer of the machine. In a similar vein, philosopher William Barrett observes that "the computer only gives us back ourselves. It is a faithful mirror that reflects the human traits that are brought to it . . . there could be other human faces that the computer might give back to us — the face of arrogance, of ruthlessness, of the lust for power." A similar point to that made by Barrett is dramatized in Joseph and Karel Capek's famous play, *R.U.R.*

It is reasonable to assume that the Capek brothers, who were from Prague, were influenced by the Golem legend when they wrote their play *R.U.R.* It is in this work that the term "robot" was coined. "Robot" derives from a Czech root meaning a "worker" in the sense of a slave laborer.

R.U.R. is the abbreviation for "Rossum's Universal Robots." The play takes place at an R.U.R. factory that manufactures robots. In the course of the play, the robots take over both the factory and the world. After the robots have all but annihilated the human race, Alquist, a clerk at the R.U.R. factory, asks the robots, "Why did you murder us?" Radius, one of the robots, replies, "Slaughter and domination are necessary if you want to be like men. Read history, read the human books. You must domineer and murder if you want to be like men." In other words, artificially created beings only reflect their creators. The evil a machine may do only reflects back upon its creator. The artificial beings we create can tell us as much about human nature as about the nature of technology or of machines. Creation of a Golem is not only an expression of human achievement, but an exercise — sometimes a horrifying one — in human self-understanding. Our fear of the results of technological achievement is simply a reflection of our fear of ourselves. This fear may not be an unjustified fear. The threat of nuclear war indicates in a shockingly real way that the Golems we create to defend us may ultimately destroy us. The explosion of technology since the Industrial Revolution may indicate to us that the more exposure to machines we experience, the more we may tend to define ourselves and to think of ourselves as machines. Machines may not only reflect human proclivities, but they may cause us to alter the manner in which we think of human nature, of ourselves.

43

In this regard, Karl Marx's observation has become increasingly accurate. In 1844 Marx warned that "as machines become more human, men will become more like machines" (*Economic and Philosophical Manuscripts*).

On the basis of Marx's observation, one may claim that the proclivity in modern western thought to define the human being as a kind of machine, and, conversely, to grant human status to certain kinds of machines, is based upon a mechanistic and physicalist view of reality that is reductionalist in nature and in approach. This philosophic tendency obscures the spiritual dimension of the human creature and treats the category of uniqueness as a superfluous bother. However, because this attitude has become so deeply engrained in modern western thought, it bears discussion.

One of the traits unique to human beings is the endeavor of self-definition. Only human beings define themselves. How we define ourselves reflects what we think of ourselves, how we view ourselves. Beginning in the eighteenth century it became fashionable to define the human being as a kind of machine. Once internalized, this philosophical position becomes a determining factor in human behavior. Once accepted by the individual, this philosophical assumption becomes a psychological presupposition.

In the seventeenth century the eminent philosopher, Rene Descartes, introduced a distinction between "thinking beings" and "extended beings." He classified human beings as uniquely self-conscious thinking beings. For Descartes, animals were "extended beings." Descartes described animals as automata. In the eighteenth century, the French philosopher La Mettrie rejected Descartes' position out of hand. According to La Mettrie, human beings are also machines. In his work, *Man, A Machine (L'Homme Machine)*, La Mettrie described the human body as "a machine that winds its own springs."

La Mettrie's view was expanded by Mechanist and Materialist philosophers and thinkers who came after him. For example, in the nineteenth century, the atheist philosopher, Robert Ingersoll, observed that "man is a machine into which we put what we call food and produce what we call thought." In other words, humans are thinking machines. The novelist Isak Dinesen went further in writing, "What is man when you come to think about him, but a minutely set, ingenious machine for turning, with infinite artfulness, the red wine of Shiraz into urine?" In the early twentieth century, an American philosopher defined the human being as "an ingenious array of portable plumbing."

From the conception of the self as a variety of machine, it is an easy jump for one's behavior to become machine-like. In this regard, for example, consider the following description by Jerzy Kosinski (*Passion Play*):

> They appeared to him, most of them, to have consented to the manufacture of their lives at some common mint, each day struck from the master mold, without change, a duplicate of what had gone before and was yet to come. Only some accident could bring to pass upheaval in the unchallenged round of their lives.
>
> It was not contempt he felt for them, merely regret that they had allowed the die of life to be cast so early and so finally. He preferred individuals whose singularity gave him insight into himself. . . . people (are) so programmed to be efficient, civil, ready with a practiced smile, that the very juices of life had been leeched from their bodies. Like the cash machines that were posted in the bank lobbies . . . the men and women who worked in banks were to Fabian as functional as the currency itself . . .

It is all but inevitable that once internalized, the notion of the human being as a variety of machine would influence our self-understanding, our attitude towards ourselves, and our behavior towards others. Even our daily colloquial speech has been influenced by the conception of the human person as a variety of machine. For example, we talk of ourselves as being "turned on" and "turned off." We "tune in" and "tune out." We provide "input" and "output." We go on vacations to "recharge our batteries." We "gear ourselves up" and "get our motors running" at the beginning of a day. By the end of a day we are "wound up," and so we must "unwind."

Even our sexual lives, our most intimate experiences, are influenced by technological thought, by the notion that the human being is a kind of machine. A basic notion of technological thought is that mastery of the proper technique will insure a solution to any given problem. One only need find the right method, and all problems in life will inevitably yield before it. The widespread acceptance of this notion accounts for the flood of "how to" manuals. We tacitly assume that the right method will inevitably produce the desired results. The inevitable consequence of this approach when applied to sexuality is that sex comes to be thought of mainly as problem of method and of technique. While Plato defined love as "madness," we tend to define love in terms of "method." Sex thereby becomes technique-centered rather than person-centered. Psychologist Rollo May has termed this view "salvation through technique."

According to May the emphasis upon technique, when carried beyond a certain point, makes for a mechanistic attitude towards love-making. One begins to think of oneself as a machine. One begins to use one's body as a machine. "Performance" and "function" come to supersede feeling and emotion. Sex becomes "product" oriented. Achieving orgasm — the product of sexual technique — becomes the *primary* goal of sexual activity. The goal becomes being a great performer. The emphasis shifts from pleasure to performance. In May's words, "The Victorian person sought to

have love without falling into sex; the modern person seeks
to have sex without falling into love" (*Love and Will*, p. 46).
The goal becomes "Making oneself feel less in order to per-
form better!" (Ibid, p. 55).

As sex education achieves growing acceptance, this
mechanistic attitude is often conveyed to the next generation. As theologian-psychologist Sam Keen has written:

> Most love-talk quickly passes over into a discus-
> sion of techniques and morality of the sexual act.
> In spite of efforts of the neo-Victorians, sex edu-
> cation is taking its place in the curriculum. And
> should it fail to receive formal status, adequate
> textbooks are available at any drugstore, and op-
> portunities for on-the-job training are not want-
> ing. Unfortunately, most sex education deals
> largely with how babies are made, diseases avoid-
> ed, or orgasms produced. And the study of the
> geography of the erogenous zones may make sex
> a matter of genital engineering in which anxiety
> over performance replaces the sweet pandemon-
> ium of love. Acquiring living habits and attitudes
> requires more than a study of the technology of
> arousal (*To A Dancing God*, p. 58).

What novelist Kosinski and psychologist May attack is
the trivialization of human uniqueness, the dehumanization
of individual human sanctity, the self-negation of being
human that accompanies a human being's acquiescence —
explicitly or implicitly — to the definition of the human being as a variety of machine. (See also the similar views of
theologians Abraham Joshua Heschel — *Who Is Man?*,
Sam Keen — *To A Dancing God*, and philosopher William
Barrett — *Time of Need* and *The Illusion of Technique*.)

In his novel *The Golem*, Gustav Meyrink warns us of the
danger of "humans to dwindle to soulless entities so soon
as was extinguished within them some slightest spark of

47

an idea." Like Kosinski and May, Meyrink issues a not so gentle admonition. At a time when Golems populate our daily lives, at a time when we must relate to machines on a daily basis, the challenge before us is not how to build bigger and better Golems, but how to prevent ourselves from becoming Golems and from having our lives controlled or even harmed by the Golems we have created.

What the Golem legend can teach us is that the Golem, the machine, while not human, is nevertheless a reflection of the best and the worst of that which makes us human. The potential harm and terror with which contemporary Golems can afflict us is but the reflection of our own penchant for self-harm and for self-destruction. The potential of the Golem to wreak havoc and destruction and the consequent need for the Golem's potential destructiveness to be recognized and controlled offers us a serious warning to temper our own destructiveness and that of the many powerful Golems we have created.

Meyrink, Kosinski and others offer a warning while they pose a challenge. The warning is that if we conceive of ourselves as machines, then we become like machines — devoid of freedom, creativity and spontaneity; we become soulless mechanical entities. We regress from the status of human being back to the golemic state; we chose thereby to evolve backwards. For these writers, and for others, the pressing problem is not whether Golems can be considered as humans, but how to prevent humans from becoming as Golems. The challenge they pose is the pressing need for human beings to intensify their quest to realize and to manifest those essentially human qualities that ultimately distinguish us from the Golems we have created. In this view, the omnipresence of Golems in our daily lives offers us a challenge to become more intensely human in order to accentuate those characteristics that make us peculiarly human and which can promise to liberate us from the proto-human golemic state to which we have a tendency to regress.

The choice — conscious or unconscious — to revert to the golemic state is not an irreversible one. Human regression — spiritual or psychological — to the golemic state can become an opportunity for each person to do with him/herself that which God did to the first Golem that became the first human. In the talmudic account, it is God who transforms Adam-Golem into Adam-Human. It is God who transmutes the Golem into an ensoulled person capable of celebrating his/her creative freedom and his/her sacred individuality. Now, not only the ability to create Golems from the elements, but also the possibility of transforming ourselves from golemic potentiality to human actuality is within our own grasp.

The Golem provides us with a mirror image of what we once were, but it also offers us a window through which we can perceive — both the promise and the horror — of what we are able to become. Ultimately, what distinguishes us from the Golem, from the machine, is our ability freely to choose the image of ourselves that we wish to become and can become.

Bibliography

Anderson, Alan, ed. *Minds and Machines*. New Jersey: Prentice Hall, 1964.

Ashkenazi, Zevi. *Responsa*. Amsterdam, 1812.

Barrett, William. *The Illusion of Technique*. New York: Doubleday, 1978.

———————————— *Time of Need*. New York: Harper, 1973.

Bin Gorion, Emanuel, ed. *Mimekor Yisrael: Classical Jewish Folktales*. 3 vols. Philadelphia: Jewish Publication Society, 1976.

Bloch, Chaim. *Der Prager Golem*. Berlin, 1920. English trans., *The Golem of Prague*, trans. by H. Schneiderman. Vienna: Vernay, 1925.

Bokser, Ben Zion. *From the World of the Cabbalah: The Philosophy of Rabbi Judah Loew of Prague*. New York: Philosophical Library, 1954.

Borges, Jorge Luis, "The Golem," *A Personal Anthology*. New York: Grove Press, 1967.

Brod, Max. *Tycho Brache's Weg Zu Gott*. Munich, 1915.

Brotman, Harris. "Human Embryo Transplants," *New York Times Magazine*. January 8, 1984.

Capek, Joseph, and Capek, Karel, trans. R. Selver. *R.U.R.* London: Oxford University Press, 1961.

Cherfas, Jeremy. *Man-Made Life*. New York: Pantheon, 1982.

Ciadin, Martin. *Cyborg*. New York: Warner, 1972.

Dan, Joseph. *Torat Ha-Sod Shel Hasidut Ashkenaz*. Jerusalem: Bialik Institute, 1968.

Davidson, Avram, "The Golem," in ed. J. Dann. *Wandering Stars*. New York: Harper and Row, 1974.

Del Zio vs. *Presbyterian Hospital,* 74 Civ. 3588, New York City.

Diamond vs. *Chakrabarty,* 447 U.S. 303 (1980).

Dreyfus, Hubert. *What Computers Can't Do: The Limits of Artificial Intelligence.* New York: Harper, 1979.

Emden, Jacob. *Megillat Sefer.* Warsaw, 1896.

_____ *She'elat Yaavetz.* Altona, 1739.

Fletcher, Joseph. *The Ethics of Genetic Control.* New York: Doubleday, 1974.

Gaylin, Willard. "We Have the Awful Knowledge to Make Exact Copies of Human Beings." *New York Times Magazine,* March 6, 1972.

Geduld, H.M. and Gottesman, R., eds. *Robots.* Boston: Little Brown, 1978.

Goldsmith, Arnold L. *The Golem Remembered, 1909-1980.* Detroit: Wayne State University Press, 1981.

Gonen, Jay Y. *A Psychohistory of Zionism.* New York: Meridian, 1975.

Goodfield, June. *Playing God: Genetic Engineering and Manipulation of Life.* New York: Harper and Row, 1977.

Gottesdeiner, A., "Ha-Ari She-be-Hakhme Prag," *Azkara III.* ed. J.L. Fishman. Jerusalem, 1937.

Grun, Nathan. *Der Hohe Rabbi Low und sein Sagenkreis.* Prague, 1885.

Hook, Sidney, ed. *Dimensions of Mind.* New York: Collier, 1961.

Howard, Ted and Rifkin, Jeremy. *Who Should Play God?* New York: Dell, 1977.

Ish-Kishor, Shulamit. *The Master of Miracle.* New York: Harper and Row, 1971.

Israel, Richard. "Make Your Own Golem." *Religious Education.* January 1981, 76:1, pp. 64-70.

Jonas, Hans. "Biological Engineering." In *Philosophical Essays.* New Jersey: Prentice Hall, 1974.

Judson, Horace F., *The Eighth Day of Creation.* New York: Simon and Schuster, 1979.

Kanter, Shammai, "If Man Creates Life Is He Still Man?" *National Jewish Monthly,* November 1963.

Kaplan, Aryeh. *Meditation and Kabbalah.* Maine: Weiser, 1982.

Keane, Noel. *The Surrogate Mother.* New York: Everest House, 1981.

Keen, Sam. *To A Dancing God.* New York: Harper, 1970.

Klatzkin, Jacob. *Thesaurus Philosophicus.* 2nd ed: New York: Feldheim, 1968.

Koestler, Arthur. *The Ghost in the Machine.* New York: Macmillan, 1967.

Kosinski, Jerzy. *Passion Play.* New York: Bantam, 1980.

Leiner, Gerson Hanokh. *Sidrei Taharot.* Pietrokov, 1903.

Leivick, H. (Leivick Halper). *The Golem.* trans. Joseph C. Landis in *Great Jewish Plays.* New York: Avon, 1972, pp. 217-356.

Levin, Ira. *The Boys from Brazil.* New York: Dell, 1976.

Lion, A.J. and Lukas, J. *Das Prage Ghetto.* Prague, 1959.

Loew, Judah ben Bezalel. *Be'er Ha-Golah.* Prague, 1598. New York, 1969.

_____ *Hiddushei Aggadot.* New York, 1969.

McDermott, Beverly Brodsky. *The Golem.* New York: Lippincott, 1976.

May, Rollo. *Love and Will.* New York: Norton, 1969.

Meyrink, Gustav. *Der Golem.* Eng. trans. by M. Pemberton. Boston: Houghton Mifflin, 1928.

Ozick, Cynthia. "Puttermesser and Xanthippe," in *Levitation.* New York: Knopf, 1982.

Peretz, I.L. "The Golem." trans. I. Howe, in ed. Howe and Greenberg. *A Treasury of Yiddish Stories.* New York: Viking, 1954.

"Popsicle Babies." *Parade,* July 10, 1983.

President's Commission for the Study of Ethical Problems in Medicine and Biomedical and Behavioral Research. *Splicing Life: The Social and Ethical Issues of Genetic Engineering with Human Beings*. Washington: U.S. Government Printing Office, 1982.

Rifkin, Jeremy. *Algeny*. New York: Viking, 1983.

Rorvik, David. *In His Image: The Cloning of a Man*. New York: Lippincott, 1978.

Rosenberg, Yudl. *Nifla'ot Maharal im ha-Golem*. Warsaw, 1909. Eng. trans. in ed. J. Neugroschel, *Yenne Velt: The Great Works of Jewish Fantasy and the Occult*. New York: Stonehill, 1976.

Rosenfeld, Albert. *The Second Genesis*. Englewood Cliffs, N.J.: Prentice Hall, 1969.

Rosenfeld, Azriel. "Generation, Gestation and Judaism." *Tradition 12:1 (1971), pp. 79-87*.

_____ "Human Identity: Halakhic Issues." *Tradition* 15:3 (1977), pp. 58-75.

_____ "Judaism and Gene Design." *Tradition* 13:2 (1972), pp. 71-81.

_____ "Religion and the Robot." *Tradition 8:3 (1966), pp. 15-27*.

Rosenfeld, Beate. *Die Golemsage und ihr Verwertung in der deutschen Literatur*. Breslau, 1934.

Rosner, Fred. "Artificial Insemination in Jewish Law." *Judaism 19:4 (Fall 1970), pp. 452-465*.

Rothberg, Abraham. *The Sword of the Golem*. New York: 2nd ed. Bantam Books, 1971.

Ruggill, Peter. *The Return of the Golem: A Chanukah Story*. New York: Holt, Rinehart and Winston, 1979.

Saul, John. *The God Project*. New York: Bantam Books, 1983.

Scholem, Gershom. "The Golem of Prague and the Golem of Rehovot." In *The Messianic Idea in Judaism*. New York: Schocken, 1971.

_____ "The Idea of the Golem." trans. R. Manheim, in *On The Kabbalah and Its Symbolism*. New York: Schocken, 1965.

Scholem, Gershom. *Kabbalah.* New York: Quadrangle, 1974.

Sefer Ha Bahir. Eng. trans. Aryeh Kaplan, *The Bahir.* Maine: Weiser, 1979.

Sefer Yetzirah. Eng. trans. Knut Stenring. 2nd ed: New York: Ktav, 1970.

Shannon, Thomas A., ed. *Bioethics.* New York: Paulist Press, 1976.

Shapira, Zvi Hirsch. *Darkhei Teshuvah.* Jerusalem: 1967.

Sherwin, Byron L. *Mystical Theology and Social Dissent: The Life and Works of Judah Loew of Prague.* London: Associated University Presses, 1982.

Siegel, Seymour. "Genetic Engineering." *Proceedings of the Rabbinical Assembly, 1978.* New York: The Rabbinical Assembly, 1978, pp. 164-167.

Simons, Geoff. *Are Computers Alive?* Boston: Birkhauser, 1983.

Singer, Isaac Bashevis. *The Golem.* New York: Farrar, Straus and Giroux, 1982.

Stein, A. *Die Geschichte der Juden in Bohmen.* Brunn, 1904.

Thieberger, Fredrick. *The Great Rabbi Loew of Prague.* London: East-West Library, 1955.

Trachtenberg, Joshua. *Jewish Magic and Superstition.* New York: Behrman House, 1939.

Varga, Andrew C. *The Main Issues in Bioethics.* New York: Paulist Press, 1980.

Veatch, Robert M. *Case Studies in Medical Ethics.* Cambridge, Mass.: Harvard University Press, 1977.

Watson, James. "Moving Toward Clonal Man." *Atlantic Monthly.* 227 (May 1971), pp. 50-53.

Wiener, Norbert. *God and Golem, Inc.* Cambridge, Mass.: MIT Press, 1964.

Wiesel. Elie. *The Golem.* New York: Summit Books, 1983.

Winkler, Gershon. *The Golem of Prague.* New York: Judaica, 1980.